Love on the Menu

Lila Vex

Published by Lila Vex Publishing, 2024.

LOVE ON THE MENU

First edition. June 10, 2024.

Copyright © 2024 Lila Vex.

ISBN: 979-8990544239

Written by Lila Vex.

To my dear readers, thank you for your unwavering support, for embracing my stories, and for joining me on this literary journey. Your enthusiasm and encouragement mean the world to me. This book is dedicated to you, the ones who bring these words to life.

CHAPTER 1

So goes the saying: once you get a taste of something, it stays with you. I never question it, for from the first day I set foot in a professional kitchen, I knew that's what I was meant to do. Since my childhood, I've remembered this uncontrollable desire of flavor matching, of plating, and of that happiness surrounding me with an invisible aura while observing someone eating a dish made by me from all my love and soul—the memories that have always been the pillar of the fire for this culinary craft.

Honestly, I'm not sure that I remember the exact moment I fell in love with cooking, but there was always a thought that passed vividly through my mind. How could the simple ingredients, with the alchemy that is cooking, be turned into something miraculous? I would spend afternoons trying to create culinary masterpieces in the Everling kitchen. Unbelievable was this sense among my senses: crunching the sound of vegetables being freshly cut, the smell of zestful herbs, and, finally, that magical sizzle of the pan. And it was exactly during such moments that I felt and knew who I am: I need to set new standards in the cooking world, and in order to do just that, I had to act with complete self-reliance.

With the splendor of my 32nd year, I now own a bustling eatery where my imaginative ideas, referred to as 'food' or 'cuisine', are visually realized. I have put my heart and soul into this venture, just to list a few ways to peel off the façade and create a dining experience that leaves one breathless in both the visual and oral senses. Every time a food item departs from my kitchen, I stand proud! More than that, the dish also proves that I aim for nothing less than perfection. It's naturally there in me.

It is, for sure, much more than just a job for me. It is my way of life and my eternal passion. The drive doesn't stop; I can't let go; I have to keep searching with stubbornness for the new, for new ideas, and to extend boundaries.

And not just content with a mere copying of what already exists, I redefine the limitations of what can be done at a food level and further do this through the invention of some new varieties of flavors, textures, and presentation.

This insatiable hunger for innovation and unending passion for my craft—through thick and thin—has found me in this place within my career. The Michelin star, the most prestigious in the field of gastronomy, has been the moment of my life—the realization of my dream—and my resolute toil was worth every sacrifice. I leave no stone unturned on the path to achieving this dream.

The Michelin star has been the candle of hope, the last rekindle, and the chase in my life as a chef. Every chef aspires to have this prestigious award given only to the crème de la crème of culinary houses. It is the result of years of relentless effort and dedication that never loses a beat in pursuit of perfection.

After my first job as a chef, I aspired to reach that Michelin star and immediately gain respect, or to place myself as some sort of visionary in the tough turf of chefdom. After all, the Michelin Guide has long since been the standard for the industry. This milestone was so much more than just a system of awards that has been in place for many years. The chef has been adamant about providing the best of his wares and never fails in his service. Coming into the group of Mettezin Outryted is a single dream, and for that, the name of my restaurant is mentioned among other culinarians. It became the kind of obsession that didn't let go for a minute in awake life. All I did was just expand my abilities in the kitchen during the years of devotion and incessant determination to succeed. Each and every recipe, every dumpling wrapped in a presto, winds up being a process of refinement—a driving force behind a never-satiated appetite for perfection.

This is not a walk in the park—it is at the top level, and one has to have a forest of obstacles to climb over before being awarded the star. The commitment level and readiness to adjust according to emerging trends and changed taste buds should be very high.

This is a challenge that I have definitely internalized and taken with all my fiber and muscle since, with a star earned, it will be the recognition of all my relentless efforts for this life mission of reaching perfection in gastronomy but also a cause for my restaurant to have the upper hand in the business. In this foodservice world, there is no let-up—an unforgiving and demanding environment in which so much time is spent trying to win more recognition and awards while fighting for the loyalty of the food industry. No longer shall I be the stranger in the roughing it out and shedding the undercover once I have my own elite restaurant where it is me standing on the chef's bench as the executive chef.

The more I walk into my restaurant each day, the more of a realization I get that there are just too few but very critical challenges. The more evident is the very high extent of competition, with seasoned and amateur chefs struggling to outdo each other, and growing by the day is the desire to impress consumers with novelty and the commercial appeal of the dishes. It's a virtuous cycle of innovation, off-beat variation, and flavor, but one wrong slip is all it takes to result in your downfall.

But I wouldn't exchange that for a more rapid way.

With all of the great odds that I have up against me working in the highly demanding food industry, as clearly seen from my insatiable desire, realness, and self-belief, I just keep on keeping on, delving far deeper into the uncharted regions of the culinary world. It drives me, the hurdle of it. I draw my energy from making the most unbelievable meals and giving an impression that could be rated as heaven. Hard work has never been about being "an average student who makes straight grades." That means an all-in commitment to the field of work, the preparedness to take continuous calculated risks, and a relentless commitment to growth and development.

Every morning, I am presented with the kitchen, filled with people of like minds working together and dedicated to the place. The time and effort that we put in to make it a better work area makes it wonderful. We enter the gastronomic space of excitement and weariness, lifting ourselves together with those stones of exquisite dishes through unique culinary styles, culinary techniques, and unique ingredients, always pushing the limits of what can be done on a plate.

Pressure to perform a great meal every time and to wow every person who walks through the doors is a burden that I wear with pride. That's a lot of weight to carry. I understand that complacency is the enemy of greatness, especially in this cutthroat industry where reputations can be made or shattered in a single review. I need to be vigilant, always evolving, and never letting off the throttle of my passion.

To top it all, even my personal life has been so complicated. The fact that I am the girlfriend of Joseph Hartley, a very well-known food critic and patron of my establishment, just heightens the complexity of things that I have to face.

Hartley and I could differ on so many points, but in the class where food is placed, we are definitely birds of a feather. From that same place, born within us, is the love of blending flavors and feeling how a dish is dancing in our mouths. We are soul mates, and we share many aspects, but one thing is for sure: We cannot and are not going to stop being foodies, not going to stop looking for and finding the best gazpacho ever.

However, there is a glass veneer of our joint sentiments, within which there is a basic conflict of opinions that has made the air heavy, emerging from the backdrop of our interactions. Joseph is very fond of the old times and old cooking techniques, so it does not always appear very good to me when, in an obvious manner, I irritate him by bringing in some fresh thinking and new elements of cuisine in my take on things.

This, to me, is just a way of capturing the uneven tone of jazz through improvisations and rhythms and very much missing out on the greatness of its purest form. While he worships the proven, the person that I am is urged to forge new ground and tear down barriers of achievability in the cooking circle. That way, the different viewpoints drag me into a race to see which one of them I end up dealing with while dealing with the obstacles that pose a threat to my campaign.

Since he is a critic, Hartley has not hesitated to criticize me in his show, in which he always either puts up or pulls down my restaurant.

He threw a stone at my audacious presentations, at my not following the traditional rules of fine dining, and at my nonconforming taste combinations. Where he restored dreams of mine, I now breed burning ambitions to guard with its heart my cuisine, to take it firmly into my arms, and into defiance of the end. Hartley's philosophy versus mine has been the prime stage in my hunt for a Michelin star—a trophy for which he has never hidden his belief that I have no business even going for in my career.

The crushing critiques he made had the power to level all my striving for success and left me wondering if the finely crafted and beautiful confections I created for guests held any value at all if that value could be reduced to a critic's whim.

I hate him, and I blame him for it, yet he still occupies my imagination. Well, that only shows how he had an effect on my life. Still, if I had to choose, I would go for tradition and not for anything modern, for it is his unrelenting expectations and his determination not to come down from his all-time BST that make me go on learning and reaching ever higher on the ladder to deliver another culinary masterpiece. The one characteristic that makes me so different as a chef is the boundless love and unyielding pride that I put into literally every item that I prepare. Championship drive and the determination to achieve far more than expected in the kitchen are words that would hardly describe the personality I possess, but what would make them whole would be the burning temperament inside of me.

It goes to show that I would go for the jugular of anybody who might dispute the integrity of my dishes.

For me, the ability to cook is not a profession but a warm inclination. This is my lifelong obsession—one that pushes me to mad passion. Every flavor, every texture, and every perfectly timed, meticulous combo is my representation of who I am. The hours and hours of practice that have shaped me, the determination to break barriers in the kitchen, and the constant work that I put in to get it right. But if their honesty is doubted, just like Joe Hartley, the great food critic, who dared to attack in words at the very center of my culinary vision, then I ascend on the very mountain, becoming a volcano with fumes of revenge entangled in chains of anger. I'm also very much immediately on the defense of my works, being very resilient in the face of literally any force that can press downwards on the true passion I'm putting into them.

It's the characteristic of my personality that was the driver of all my successes, and sometimes it drove me over the edge.

Of course, I cannot help but admit the fact that it is this amazing energy, which this passion gives me, that has allowed me to be "a star" of the cooking world. I have come to be known as a master of my craft who dares to make things that were not made or were considered impossible some time ago.

However, to some extent, this over-protectiveness, resilience, and indifference in front of people have also resulted in the need for Joseph Hartley at a distance and his resentful reviews that easily break our recent position and success. It will be a struggling journey to sail this ship, as the food service industry is the one that has to color this balanced line between my strengths and my weaknesses. In this desperate situation, these values keep me going: I keep alive my unvanquished weaknesses while serving the customers with the best quality of culinary. To me, being undefeated in life is not a goal but a way of life, never-ending effort in which the weight of the whole world rests, and that which drives me through even when adversities hit me.

CHAPTER 2

It should have been one of my normal nights at my place—the kind of night when I worked—but instead, the place was quiet. The constant buzz was living in the air, but the smells of fine dishes were missing. My partner and I were in the midst of it and soldiering through it; at that very moment, we were the well-oiled machine that exclusively served the food of our demanding customers.

As was his habit, there was no one who merged with the crowd so naturally—Joseph Hartley, a food critic whose dictums would long outlive a restaurant's glory or put warning to go extinct.

A man in modest and gentlemanly disguise sat glued to his seat, facing me, observing the connection of my busboys, the formality of my preparation, and the perfect presentation of every dish that came out of the kitchen. Hartley worked hard to figure out where I had slipped. Whether he knew it or not, my most-feared opponent was now sitting among us. Each step was scrutinized with sharp eyes, matching recommendations and queries deftly to future discussions. Of course, the ending was nowhere in sight—I was doomed!

In the end, as dinner progressed, in my affected style, influenced by the way I had to confidently move into my guests' dining room, the comforting murmurs from the mouths of those who had traveled in gastro—well, it was enough for me. The one situation that was starting to turn into my one solid success was seconds from coming to a halt simply because of an obscure man sitting in the corner with his eyes boring into my kitchen counter.

I could see no trace of the man himself, though his reputation in the silent gloom weighted me. Easily, the words of Hartley could unravel all that I had tried so hard to achieve—the end of so many years of practice and loving dedication to crafting each dish that left my kitchen. And now, that same man would sit in judgment and strike at my heart with that pen.

With the final course served and the last patron departed, I could have had no idea of the storm that was brewing.

Literally, after that very night, with his review's steady drip as the media kept re-grabbing it time and again, my very thumping reality seemed to be. In his spitting words, he tarnished memories of months and years I invested in my restaurant, in the pride and joy of building it to shine.

The way Houston described my kitchen, it was as if it were a disaster area—plates not off so much as blurred, with so many colors and flavors that they negated any chance of this being a classy place to eat. He had only used words to slash away my carefully nurtured success; he even goaded me on in mockery. Not even in the least; every bit less as a chef.

But it was all the stronger, as I had to prove to myself something through the wounds that were then swollen and angry. I had to be slapped by the bitter truth: my worst enemy—the one who could walk in through that door and trample on my image—was me. Why do I, with a flick of a pen, take everything that I have built in my life so far?

As much as I read only those lines, tears started to water unknowingly in the agonies of my heart. By reading this, I just felt that Hartley was telling me exactly the problem with myself: what I was afraid of, how to face it, and what to ask myself. This simple, cherished establishment, the fruit of an unparalleled work and undeterred emotion toward the self-same, I bent over in the backwoods, owed the responsibility of making gains.

For the moment, I couldn't have cared less about all the applause and adulation, not to mention all my past victories—suddenly, they seemed really pointless.

In one word, Hartley could have shattered what took me years to build. She could have left me with nothing to offer but my vulnerability and my confused mind about my assumption that I am the best at my art. Really, it was a paradox. I would throw myself totally into everything coming out of that kitchen, driven by an irrational hunger to create, to push the limits of possibility, and to make me an explorer of new boundaries of taste and presentation.

All this lifetime's worth during my college years—all these tears, all that fire in my eyes, all that determination, and all the hopes—what for? Don't they look like rotten fruit after all?

As I reached the crossroads, the moment for the Hartley review had come, with one way leading me to the comfort of reclusion and the other calling me to squarely approach the challenge. For at the heart of my turmoil, a basic question lay: if Hartley, the wizard that he was at baking, were telling the truth, where in the world do I get my talent and success, since I have never since faced it? I could feel the weight of uncertainty on me, made up by the bow of a huge boulder. I was fighting a battle all alone, and it seemed that I was losing, with each dream of mine coming to a shattering end. But as I steeled my spirit and set my face toward the future, I knew Hartley's verdict on my fair accomplishments should not be the last time he ever made such a damaging attack. And rather than just brushing off his deadly and hurtful words and focusing on a way forward, I diverted all my energy and put in all my efforts into extending and improving my craft, and then reclaiming my place in the kitchen hierarchy.

Would I sooner face the critic, in his words, as a last ditch, knowing I may end up in the converse, an escalation of discrediting charges, in an effort to keep my dreams in place?

It was a decision that had blanketed my consciousness, being pierced by the ramifications of each of my choices that had left me at a crossroads. However transparent that judicious road may have appeared to be, I did not want to be unresponsive to Hartley's critique. And I could not brush it off my shoulder since it was the usual way of life in the world I had been a part of. So, I decide to put all my effort and resources into responding by proving to be an outstanding chef, the best there was in that world of life in the restaurants.

Well, it was critics that I had drawn in the first place, so I was thinking: if not even the opinion of the most powerful critics in this industry meant anything once their words had been scattered on the capricious wind. I will be remembered, looking back, as someone who hadn't been cowardly, as someone without a lack of resolution in his quest to become a master in the kitchen—no doubt good enough to bring me back to this somehow disappointing place and rebuild my reputation as a culinary star.

However, one side of my mind was deeply offended by the very idea of not responding to Hartley's attack; in the meantime, accepting his discouraged opinion was, from my point of view, so bitter that it was absolutely against my chef's personality. I am mad, but not as mad as I got to be for one reason: the very fabric that I worked hand in hand for years to build and the diligence and creativity that I invested were all for naught after that man pronounced a mere piece of judgment against me.

Whether I like it or not, the fact is, do I marry it up or do I just take a stand?

If you will, that wouldn't be mono, but rather broaching on the very essence of what got me this far: to forsake that stubborn pride marking my culinary style and philosophy. I felt a need for justice and revenge. The urge for retribution was so powerful, exactly in such a way that it nearly devoured all of my reason within me. Pride wrestled with that burning desire in my heart to set things right, the implications of each decision, and the potential consequences that haunted my mind one sleepless night after another. Caution, on the other hand, was the sort of response measured and weighed that focused on the long game—the slow crawl to the top.

But on the other hand, the siren call of confrontation was an opportunity to go face-to-face with Hartley's critique and stand up for the honor of my beloved establishment.

As I paced the floors of my restaurant, the familiar sights and sounds served as the perfect accompaniment to my interior tumult, and I was reminded of all I had sacrificed to this point: hours upon hours of perfecting techniques, relentless experimenting with the palette, an unwavering dedication that turned my passion into a culinary empire—all of it threatened to come undone with the stroke of Hartley's pen. And in that moment, once again, I understood it was not in me to be able to just stand by without doing something. I can't be silent. All the brickwork from the building of my dream and vision that bonded me to inner strength in the worst of situations was now disturbed. Not to back down, let this argument go unchallenged, would not be a betrayal of these words alone, but a betrayal to my very self, to the core of who I am. as an entrepreneur. It would be to surrender the same firm principles that this business is based upon.

No, I opted to direct all my energies toward that struggle, which at all costs requires a sacrifice to be made. It has always been very much of a struggle to lie down there, trying to have full control of the situation in regard to my life and career while it was at its all-time low. That the risk of being even more scrutinized in future—since I had just directly confronted the most formidable critic of culture—and the possible backlash considered nothing in the face of the fire in me, proving that my name is a reign in.

Meanwhile, all this dissimulation could not veil the commotion in me.

But valiantly, I continued my march straight ahead, for this is the only direction my dreams take. I wouldn't slink under the assault of Hartley's words. I wouldn't let his sentences wheel back and alter the nature of what I had done in that life.

I was vigilant, empowered by the resilience that got me started and the firm belief that my cooking polish would finally shine. What lay ahead was all uncertain, and the realization that I would soon be face-to-face with Hartley's stone might provide an opening for attack and interrogation. But, by all means, I was definitely not ignorant that I could not simply brush off that blow and think that the previous practices of all the rules could save me from this influential error in life. Life, for me, is the biggest investment in the world, and I will take on the challenge despite it being the last inch of my life.

CHAPTER 3

The day Hartley's review was published is forever etched in my memory—a moment when my world came tumbling down with the force of a hurricane. What was there to celebrate? It was not, apparently—a brilliant review by one of the most powerful voices in the world of cuisine. On the contrary, it was one of those moments that so brutally took you to your core.

My heart pounded as I read over the words; it was almost hard to believe what it said. The Hartley critique was everything that I had worked my heart and soul for, contained within one scathing indictment: a rain of unrelenting criticism that did not miss a single spot on the canvas of my culinary vision.

He went hammer and tongs at my style of cooking, deriding my innovation as nothing short of sheer gimmickry, without substance or purpose. The bold flavor combinations I had so painstakingly constructed, each one a mindfully orchestrated symphony of tastes and textures, whittled away to naught but bad ideas, were surely set to offend the palates of the discerning dining public.

His harshest criticism came when speaking of the presentations: a scathing review of the art I had woven into every plate with which I had left my kitchen. Hartley painted the picture of haphazard arrangements: arrangements not holding an ounce of coherence or appeal to the eye; in contrast, I saw thoughtful, evocative compositions in my mind's eye, each as a love letter to the senses.

Moving on through the text, my disbelief quickly twisted into a gut-wrenching, hair-raising anger that flowed through my veins like molten lava. Really, who does he think he is, throwing aside my life's work with such insouciance? Does he have any notion of how many hours I worked on my craft, not sleeping, and perfecting recipes to take them just beyond what is currently being done?

At that moment, I felt like I had really let myself down—that the very man whose approval I so desired had now turned his back on me, casting aside my culinary vision as just a passing fancy.

Beyond the anger and disbelief, a more insidious emotion threatened to consume me—fear. His words carried a weight far beyond simple criticism. With every blistering line, I could feel the foundations of my hard-earned reputation crumbling and the dreams I had so carefully nurtured slipping through my fingers.

The Michelin star that I so desperately wanted, the elusive prize that had driven me with every fiber of my being, now seemed a far-off mirage, a dream that had been wrested away through Hartley's pen stroke. I already saw the weak-willed elite of the industry, who fawned on every word of the critic's acerbic review and, hence, transferred their loyalty away from me and the culinary dream I had given so much to fulfill, turning away.

In those dark moments, as the weight of Hartley's words threatened to crush me beneath their force, I found myself teetering on the edge of despair. Have I been deluding myself all this while, running after a dream that has been jinxed not to happen? Was my pursuit of culinary excellence just a fool's errand—forever being overshadowed by the judgments of those who could never truly understand the depths of my passions?

But even as these doubts swirled within me, one ember of defiance was fanned into flame by Hartley's blistering critique—a resolution that burned red-hot and could not be quenched. I've put too much of myself into this dream, given too much, to simply let go because of one man's opinion, influential as he may be and biting in his words.

I found myself at an impasse with a decision that defined who I was as a cook. It seemed I could either take his damning words to heart, fade into the shadows, or lick my wounds—thereby letting his critique become the final word on my culinary abilities. However, that way simply was not going to cut it for me—an absolute betrayal to everything

I had fought for, every single ounce of blood, sweat, and tears I poured into my craft.

Feelings of pride were seething in me like a chef, and just an indestructible belief in the uprightness of my culinary vision wouldn't let me take the scalding Hartley appraisal by its face value. It won't be about the reputation or awards; it would be a fight for the very soul of my work in life—a fight that I would choose.

With the embers of my anger still burning bright, there was a full-fledged fire of defiance for vindication, a fire fed by an all-consuming need to make Hartley eat the truth he so flippantly defecated on: that my innovation, this push with flavors and presentations, was not a gimmick but rather lived on as the very soul of a culinary philosophy that challenged the status quo.

I could almost feel it on my tongue—a searing thirst for retribution that could be quenched by nothing less than the gratification of seeing Hartley acknowledge the artistry he had so flagrantly dismissed. For too long, I slaved over his work from the shadows of his lofty perch, attempting to seek his favor, only to be met with sheer contempt and ridicule.

No more.

It was about time to take a stand and demand the reckoning that I so richly deserved. That was the moment when determination turned into obstinacy, almost to the level of an obsession, grabbing at every conscious thought and driving me with an intensity that would simply not leave me in peace.

I will trace this elusive critic, this judge of the culinary experts who had so audaciously assaulted the very foundation of my dreams. No stone will go unturned, no lead too faint to follow, as I pursue a pursuit that brings me to the fringe of the culinary world and back.

A fever almost bordering on madness burned within my veins as I scoured to the very ends of this industry in pursuance, sifting through both whispers and rumors, chasing fleeting glimpses of Hartley's presence much like a bloodhound on the hottest of trails. With each dead end and false lead that I came to, it only served to further my resolve and fuel an insatiable thirst for demanding answers that had eluded me for far too long.

The pursuit left me with no sleep, no sustenance, and any vestige of a normal life in my unrelenting pursuit to bring Hartley to account. The burning need to clear my name, to prove to the world—and Hartley himself—that my culinary vision was not folly but a masterpiece deserving veneration and respect, formed the edge of my resolve and cut me through whatever distractions and frailties I had in those days.

On those feverish days and sleepless nights, I could feel the ambition bearing down on me all the time, a constant reminder of what was at stake. For it was no longer a mere clash of two people but a clash of two ideals—a war torn on the very basis of what it meant to be a culinary artist.

The trail grew ever hotter; the faint whispers coalesced into a clear path before me, and I knew the reckoning was at hand. Soon, I was going to look into the eyes of that man who had the audacity to challenge the very core of my existence, and when that moment came, I would be ready—like a soldier—with the full impact of my passion, my faith, and my unyielding belief in the truth that Hartley had so horribly desecrated.

For in that battle, in that fiery interchange of wills, I would come out victorious, not only for myself but for the entirety of my culinary belief. Hartley would be made to see the fault in his own ways, to see the genius he had been so blind to.

Single-mindedly, with determination not far from obsession, I pursued this Joseph Hartley with all of my might. It was such a big task to find his whereabouts, one so huge that it bordered on an inferno of obsession limbo—a maze of the culinary netherworld in which every turn tested my steely resolve.

This search, from the very start, was to be filled with exasperation and failure. It was full of dead ends and false trails, like some masochistic jigsaw puzzle, that taunted me with brief, partial glimpses of Hartley's existence only to have them yanked away, providing a cruel mirage. Reports that he was turning up at some fancy event or being sighted in some renowned culinary enclaves would prompt me to hop down the proverbial rabbit hole, with each one sucking me further into another demoralizing dead end.

I just didn't know how to give up in the face of innumerable setbacks. I got this feeling, innumerable times, of being so close to catching my quarry, only to have him slip through my fingers again. The bright belief that burned in my heart like the sun fueled my unflagging persistence: one day, somehow, sometime, I would lay hands on that damn elusive critic and ask for the accounting he so well owed.

I was like a woman possessed—sacrificing sleep, sustenance, and any semblance of a normal life in service to my singular obsession. Passion was the fuel behind a churning haze, allowing little else to enter its field of vision as it drove from one chase to the next. My very restaurant—the zenith, the concrete dream of all my culinary aspirations—faded into the background as I gave my every drop of blood to the hunt for Hartley.

Every day that passed, it seemed to weigh heavier, like an anvil that no one could lift—a constant reminder of just exactly what was at stake due to this gambit of my ambition. Now the prize and the reputation did not matter; it was now a battle for the very soul of my craft, an ideology to be drawn into—a headlong collision of world-shaping ideologies that would shape my destiny and my indelible stamp upon the world.

And so I pressed on, unrelenting to the obstacles in my way, powered by the flames of my belief and the knowledge that victory is just a matter of keeping at it. I trawled really every corner of the sector; no stone was left unturned, and no lead, however feeble, was left out in the quest.

Finally, after what had seemed like hours of fruitless searching, a faint glimmer of hope appeared.

That was where the first rumors of the high society of the culinary event, supposedly the most prestigious get-together for everyone involved with this sphere, had it that the ever-elusive Hartley would grace their event. This was the break that I had been looking for feverishly, the opportunity that I had been chasing to the darkest corners of the culinary world.

Then, there was a new purpose I let out in pursuit, my heart thumping with new feelings—expectation and dread. This was the moment I had waited for—the chance to meet the man who had changed my world, the man whose very words had threatened to unravel the very fabric of my dreams.

With each stride toward my victim, the burden of the impending confrontation weighed down upon me so heavily, an almost tangible burden that seemed to have the power to crush me underfoot. I would not be cowed; I would refuse to yield to the fear and doubt that niggled at the edges of my resolution.

For it was then that I became not only a chef but a warrior, a culinary titan ready to go into battle—the greatest battle of all time, a clash of wills and ideas that would change the course of my career and the legacy I would live for in the world.

So, all set for that eye-to-eye he had been itching for, I was ready for the firestorm, fully armed to the teeth with the power of my passion and belief—in a belief that had become undisturbed even by the truth, so brutally flung away by Hartley.

It was the moment of reckoning for which I had been in a fever of anticipation—the crucible in which I would either emerge victorious, vindicating the integrity of my culinary vision, or be forever consigned to the shadows of Hartley's scathing verdict.

I knew that if I went down, so be it, but I was not going to go down without a fight.

There was an electric charge of recognition when I saw Joseph Hartley, as if the atmosphere itself were charged with our collision, to take place in a second. It had been months of relentless pursuit, gnawing doggedness, and single-minded obsession that had brought me to this point—a meeting with the man whose scathing words had threatened to put asunder the very fabric of my culinary dreams.

Staring into each other's eyes, I could feel simmering tensions between us building up over all too long a time, finally reaching their boiling point. Within that moment, the weight of our opposing philosophies—our clashing ideologies—seemed to hang in the air like a suffocating shroud over the both of us, threatening to consume us both in a firestorm of long-simmering resentment and wounded pride.

His saying was that the instant Hartley opened his mouth, it was as though the dam had broken loose, and a torrent of pent-up fury spilled out in a searing, take-no-prisoners exchange that rocked to the very foundation of the culinary world. In that moment, we were titans colliding, two immovable forces locked in a battle for the very soul of our craft—a clash that would end up determining the course of our futures and the indelible marks we would leave upon the world. Ever the flag-bearer of convention and the sturdy follower of the safe path, Hartley let me have it: a blistering assault against my avant-garde approach, nay, my boundary-pushing culinary vision, which could only be termed a misplaced folly. It was said in an acrimonious tone, each word like a poisoned dart, purposely meant to sink deeply into the very core of my innovation.

I was no willow, no frail petal to be overturned by the storm in his critique. No, I was a force of nature, a hurricane in the culinary world borne on the wings of unbridled passion that had brought me to this instant in time, and I was not going to be put off in any sense of the word.

But then I felt, with a ferocity that appeared to shake the very walls around us, that I let loose a torrent of my own in defense, a staunch defense for the integrity of my artistry, the careful orchestration of flavors and textures that had become the hallmark of my avant-garde approach. Not for the sake of a few, but I related to them as the very building blocks of my culinary philosophy, disclosing in me the intensity of that drive for continuous innovation, an unsatisfiable quest to have new boundaries in every other field.

Every single word, every ardent plea, was a clarion call; each statement was one that what I saw was no mere vision, but the very heart and soul of a culinary revolution, the turn of the paradigm in what it meant to be a chef, an artist, a visionary.

Our voices crescendoed to a fever pitch, clashing against one another, never actually retreating or surrendering, like philosophies on tectonic plates, sending shockwaves through the culinary world. Hartley's respect for tradition was at war with my unapologetic pursuit of the avant-garde, his immovable object, meeting the unstoppable force of my creativity.

But no longer was I going to sit back and just defend the vision; I wanted answers, to be able to explain the scathing critique that had struck so deeply, threatening to undermine the very base of all that I had fought so hard to build.

I forced Hartley to confront the brutal disregard he'd had for my artistry—the nonchalant dismissal of the passion and dedication that fueled each moment—with a flare that outshone the same sun, I laid wide open the tattered pride that had driven me to this confrontation, the insatiable thirst for vindication that occupied every thought.

The voices, in that charged atmosphere, chimed together, and I could feel the balance of our struggle shifting. Power teetered on the precipice in the crucible of our confrontation. In the explosive exchange, the fiery collision of culinary titans, I was no longer the one to defend his vision—it was a claim to one's place among the great men, to a vision not put down too simply.

It was so much more than just a battle between two people; it was a war against the very definition of a chef, a culinary revolutionary for whom every creation was an act of rebellion against the shackles of tradition.

Our argument was rising in speed. Hartley and I were two immovable forces, our determination evenly matched as we hurled accusations and defenses across the tensely charged space between us. It was as though our explosive clash would just combust into something irreparable, just as it seemed it might, when an unexpected interruption came barreling in.

"Chefs, we need both of you in Barcelona next month at the Culinary Masters Summit," an event coordinator told us with exasperation. "You're being invited as the hosts for the opening ceremonies."

My mouth dropped open and I shot Hartley an incredulous look. Co-hosts? After everything that had gone down between us? The very idea was preposterous. An apology was already forming on my lips when the coordinator continued.

"I know that you two do not really. get along," she said hesitantly. "But you are both culinary giants. Your involvement is not only requested but will be essential to making this event a success. The eyes of the world will be watching you."

Hartley and I fired twin glares, our eyes locking in a battle of wills. Every fiber in me shrieked to decline, to get out of this somehow, to not have to endure his company one moment more than I had to. Then rationality took over; the professional in me knew that this chance was far too important to throw away over a personal vendetta. I gave a brief nod of acceptance, extremely reluctant.

A muscle twitched in Hartley's jaw, and he followed suit, his expression already painful at the prospect of our partnership. Our truce was uneasy—a brittle thing stretched to near-breaking—but the necessity of obligation held animosity at bay for a time.

CHAPTER 4

There seemed to be next to no question in my mind that the pre-summit to the Culinary Masters Summit was going to be the right spark; I just needed to really make it explode on that first ready-to-light fuse. That very same weekend later on, Hartley and I were coming back together in close quarters, marking out a team waiting for us to play professionally, deepening our problems following the wild impact that we'd had on each other, and the mere thought was again astonishing.

Whether it was the smooth lines of the boardroom or the tangible measure of the boardroom tension, I couldn't help feeling a little like Tennyson's 'third presence' of ' Old Hartley was already parked, kind of languidly sprawled over a chair, one of his ankles resting against another knee in a pushy sign of his coolness. Eyes narrow minutely over my face as I move in a little, mouth pressing into a flat line of pouting.

"And who might this Siren of the culinary mishaps be?" was amped by his obviously falsified dislike. "Apologetically, let me declare that we are here to design one hell of an avant-garde shindig."

And then I caught those sneaky words of his; they were already turning my hackles up. Through all the means possible, he would show his aversion today. This is just the same to me; I am a firestarter.

"I said in grown-up tones, with a much more subdued plan than you must have in mind. 'I touch but not lull; they are invigorated by my way to dine, though my method sometimes lulls.' "A far better thing."

That gunpowder blazed, and human skirmishing had formally begun. Then it just degenerated into one-upping the other based on a dozen irrelevant factors, from grandiose ideas down to itty-bitty details like napkin folds and charger plates. No detail was too minute or a matter of rigorous competition, and we could not compromise on anything.

"This deconstruction idiocy is just getting out of hand!" he said at one point, exploding and slamming a beefy fist down hard enough on the table to make me jump. "Guests want to be delighted and surprised when

22

they dine, not be forced to solve culinary riddles because some chef has gotten drunk on his own ego!"

"And clutching our fussy, musty old traditions to our collective bosom in total darkness is just going to strangle the life out of innovation!" I shot back across the table, right in his face. "The greats—Because, Robuchon, and Adrià—were never afraid to push the envelope and take the craft to the next level. That's what the problem is: arrogant luddites who are actually "frightened of change!"

Our words were as sharp as the battle that seemed to ensue between us, developing into an all-out battle of wits and wills in which the tension in the air was as palpable as anything. Hartley's craggy face was flushed with color, and his lips peeled back from his teeth in a sneering rictus. I was quite certain I mirrored his grimace, cheeks burning with indignant fury. We were like two forces of nature on an unstoppable collision course, neither willing to back down an inch.

How much I was completely on track at that moment, about throwing my hands in the air in pure disgust and walking out. To hell with the whole charade—how in God's name were we supposed to work like a well-oiled machine of rational professionals if we could barely make it through one meeting without resorting to bared teeth and thinly veiled insults?

But then something shifted. I saw Hartley looking at me, and something flickered over his flinty gaze. The rising urge to fling more verbal barbs faltered, brows furrowing slightly as he seemed to really look at me for the first time as something more than his maddening avant-garde foil. That ever-present sneer wavered, melting away into something entirely else.

I watched bewilderment and then comprehension dawn on his craggy features, like a veil being slowly lifted. Despite the insults and gruff exterior, at that moment, Joseph Hartley was looking at me with a newfound, almost begrudging respect. A mirror of my own dogged passion and fiery self-belief. The fight went out of him in an instant as some invisible line was crossed.

It didn't all drain from the room; this was still Hartley, after all. But it does appear like a certain amount of tension has been released from around the tightness of his jaw and the severity of his frown. Somehow, now, it was as though he was finally seeing me for the first time as a fellow artisan and peer, rather than just an arrogant nuisance to be batted away.

Perhaps in that electrified exchange, when we both laid bare our philosophies, he must have seen in me the same kind of ferocious drive for culinary brilliance that propelled his own. For all our conflicting ways of pursuing this, we were both zealots of the same religion of gastronomic perfection.

A glimmer of respect had been won in the battle. It had only been a hairline fracture in the thick walls between us, but a fracture nonetheless. And from the smallest of cracks, bigger things could eventually be swayed to emerge.

Hartley and I sat at the interminable planning meeting, the air full of tension. Ever since we were forced into this co-hosting partnership, every meeting with Hartley turns into a minefield. I have to watch each step and be careful with every word, for one single wrong step or ill-chosen word will set the whole thing off, and we may be at each other's throats again before we know it.

I swear I could see Hartley's jaw clamped so tightly that I could make out the cord of muscle jumping beneath his ruddy skin. His eyes flashed his usual contemptuous disdain at me as I settled in the chair opposite him. Hairs prickled on the back of my neck, and I knew already that my body's instinctive response to Hartley's very presence had rekindled the simmering embers of animosity between us.

"I hope you're not going to make a case for another plate of 'deconstructed potpourri' this time," he said by way of greeting, making derisive air quotes. "I'd hate for our guests to strain their jaws trying to actually find and identify the food."

I bristled at his sardonic jab, gearing up for a scathing retort, surely to fan the first skirmish of the day. And then something unexpected happened. My gaze strayed to the open kitchen just visible through the glass walls of the meeting room—the stainless steel counters gleaming, the air redolent with the mouth-watering aromas of seared foie gras and reduced demi-glace simmering on the range.

It was as if a switch had been thrown at me. Suddenly, all I could give a shit about was the culinary craft, not what petty little Hartley was trying to get me riled up about this time. In my domain, I am surrounded by all the sights, sounds, and smells that fueled my passion. It all seemed to matter less. An uneasy truce settled over me as my priorities realigned.

"Why don't we move this into the kitchen?" I heard myself suggesting in a carefully neutral tone. "It's much easier to discuss the menu and presentations when we're hands-on."

For a suspended moment, Hartley looked nonplussed at my uncharacteristic diffusion of the situation. But then his eyes strayed to the kitchen, and I watched him unclench, at least a little, under the lure of actual, real food work. Gathering his notes with a curt nod, we relocated our meeting to the culinary arena.

It was as though, after time passed, something changed. Maybe it was just me in my element, the sacred space of self, apart from the vagaries and demands of others. Maybe it was the methodical physicality of the cooking itself—the focus on one chop, slide, whisk, and stir after another—that seemed to enforce some kind of meditative trance state. At any rate, Hartley and I soon fell into step.

Gone were the harsh retorts and sneering critiques; in their place, an effortless volleying of suggestions and ideas, our frantic written notes were abandoned in place of an instructive back and forth. Add a little more of this spice for balance, and glaze with Madeira instead of Marsala for a sauce, which will heighten the nutty essence of a sauce. We would tweak and fine-tune each dish together, pulling closer and closer to absolute perfection with each one.

It is as though, in those suspended moments, the bitter feud that had characterized Hartley and me for so long was simply forgotten. Our combative energies were put on the loftier canvas of culinary brilliance; our individual strengths harmoniously merged. I watched his deft moves and supremely assured ways, enjoying his steadiness even as I might subtly push for some innovative tweak here and there.

I was seeing a side of Hartley for the first time that went beyond the gruff, acerbic persona that seemed to be his default. The man was a true master in his element at work, making even the most rudimentary of dish preparations seem startlingly spot-on yet unhurried. His hands had an economy of dreamlike motion that I was spellbound by as they worked, and I found myself not minding his presence all that much after all. If anything, he grounded me in a strange way.

With that, the combative posturing was set aside, and our clashing egos and desires to constantly one-up each other faded into the background. The intensity that took their place was shared, and Hartley and I alike brought that quality to our culinary pursuits. It was as if in these moments of collaborative preparation, all masks dropped, and we were just two artisans completely consumed by their craft.

I considered Hartley's techniques with a sort of clinical interest. No more was I to see them through the dismissive lens of antiquated traditionalism, though. Instead, I beheld the mastery and precision he commanded—the deft, nuanced flourishes and economic movements honed from decades of unwavering dedication to his craft. I had to admit there was a certain dogged beauty in his keeping to the Old World ways, even as my own impulses goaded me at each step to press for more innovative, avant-garde interpretations.

In those timeless hours of suspension, when there was no sound except the ticking of the kitchen clock, some kind of unspoken language developed between the two of us. We would shuttle back and forth in the kitchen, dancing a step and adjusting something just that infinitesimal amount closer to perfection.

A tilt of my chin and a raised brow, as if to convey the suggestion to adjust the acid balance, and sure enough, Hartley's head can ever so slightly in response, his deft hands giving the merest twisting turn of the tightening ribbon to incorporate more cream.

Our steps were perfectly in time with even the smallest of details, with both of us getting lost in the creation. Those moments were inconsequential in the face of the divisions in our dueling philosophies. Egos subsumed by the singularity of our purpose, we had become gestalt collaborators.

Every hour of it while we were there—for whole hours at a time spent in that state of pure artistic channeling—I could feel the invisible walls lowering incrementally. The taut wariness seeped from my shoulders until that ever-present tension was a distant murmur at the back of my mind. Gradually, even the combative and so-charged presence of Hartley turned almost comforting in its steady reliability. On the way, our curt answers and bitten-off retorts gave way to an easy rapport of teasing banter and wry grins. It was as though we'd found our very own shared language within which to communicate with one another through the unifying force of our culinary synergy.

I would remind him of his fusty adherence to tradition, and he would arch an eyebrow at my avant-garde flourishes done solely for shock value rather than substantive innovation. But there was no rancor behind the digs, no belittling or dismissive airs. We had become friends, I realized with a start. Of a sort, at least. Always, I had taken such pride in the rigid control and dominance of every single aspect of my kitchen realm; it was there that I reigned supreme in creative will, bending every element to my singular vision. Yet. I found myself not minding Hartley's even-keeled presence at my side through those long, fevered bursts of productivity.

If anything, his steadying influence was grounding, allowing me to stay centered even when the swirling creative tempest threatened to whip me into obsessive frenzies.

My improvisational flashes and sudden inspired detours were tempered by his measured thoughtfulness, ensuring neither of us veered too wildly in one extreme direction or another. Our various energies and incommensurate attitudes existed in one harmonious symbiosis, complimenting one another in a way never envisioned by me.

And so the hours flitted by, then days and weeks in our advanced state of culinary coexistence, and I began to brood over how divided my perceptions had once been. Hartley's more traditional philosophies didn't seem to hold quite the same air of constriction and inflexibility when I could savor, in a purely visceral sense, the technical mastery with which they were underpinned. And my own avant-garde, norm-shattering—maybe it wasn't always as radical as I had thought.

The more our ideas seeped into conversation and cross-pollinated between us, the more I saw the walls between tradition and innovation starting to get blurry. Where I had once seen the most fundamentally opposed schools of culinary thought, I now saw the opposite ends of the very same continuum of artistic expression—yin and yang, frames of reference counterbalancing one another.

Perhaps there was space within the two opposing philosophies for them to coexist after all—constantly not fighting but merging into a harmony in which light from one would reveal new sublime heights to which the other could ascend.

In the evening, the stainless steel surfaces shone dully in the harsh fluorescence of the overheads, and the kitchen remained cloaked in shadows. Most of the staff had left hours before, leaving only Hartley and me to finish preparations for tomorrow's event. An exhausted silence had descended. The prior freneticism of motion and barked orders had given way to a pensive stillness.

I went from station to station in a systematic march, constantly making small, minute changes—tweaking a garnish here and there, getting a sauce just a little bit tighter. Perfectionism was as much a part of me as my breath—along with the compulsion to always keep pushing, always present beneath the surface. The end of our day's marathon left me feeling so consumed by obsession that I had to keep going until every last piece was irrefutably, unquestionably perfect. I felt depleted to the point of exhaustion.

Hartley worked away across the kitchen with the same brand of focused intensity. There were no traces of the brusque hostility or wry baiting, so thoroughly characteristic of all our earlier interactions, emanating from him. In this sacred space that night, it seemed all pretense had been fully stripped away. We were not sworn enemies this night, nor even begrudging partners; we were just two craftsmen totally subsumed by the ritual of creation.

Hell, I'm not even sure which petty incident it was that first broke the ice between us. An agreed-upon seasoning level, perhaps, or a mild request to borrow a tool for a moment. But whatever it was, it set off the first infinitesimally small crack in the dam of formality that divided us.

In a few minutes, the tensile professionalism had yielded to the ease of a conversation drifting in quieter, more intimate waters. I should have been more on guard, more alive to the invisible lines we were so easily blurring. But in that beautiful cocoon of privacy, all the artifices fell away with every successive remark and answer.

We'd oscillate between arguing and talking about our personal lives, a conversation that extended far beyond kitchen operations and culinary ambitions. Before I had time to notice the sudden vulnerability, Hartley was already sharing what it was like growing up as the son of a single mother who was always fighting to keep their heads above water in one of Detroit's roughest neighborhoods. He learned the harsh mathematics of dividing rations to keep them fed and sacrificed parts of his own meager meals to make sure his younger siblings wouldn't get hungry. Fueling his relentless, almost to the point of obsession, pursuit of excellence in all things was that deprived youth—a firm resolve not to know such deprivation ever again.

Listening with bated breath, I could hear that boy trapped beneath Hartley's gruff exterior. The lonely striver, in whom perfection was the ultimate rebuke against the world's thousand open-cruel fists, upturned in every man's face. And in that moment of connection, I found the words spilling unbidden from my own mouth.

I've never been one to hide behind self-deprecation, but then again, I've always been open about the crippling self-doubt that haunted me like a persistent specter, no matter how many accolades and accomplishments I racked up. The nagging insecurities that cause me to endlessly second-guess each of my innovative culinary concepts, wondering if this time my ambitions had stretched too far into overindulgent gimmickry. Even at the very pinnacles of my best stretches of my career, I always felt like an impostor waiting to be unveiled as the talentless charlatan who had so far managed to bluff his way through this much.

The words came halting at first, the tight knot in my chest resisting their escape, but there was something in the steadiness and lack of flinching about Hartley that created an atmosphere of safety, I realized. There was something about his 'taking all' and 'no judgment'—something that allowed complete absorption—that let the pressure valve within fly open and allowed the freedom to be vulnerably unguarded in a way my hubris rarely allowed.

The muffled confessions flowed soon more freely, pointing to the most fragile twinges of the imposter syndrome consuming my inner psyche. I spoke of the unending desire to push my boundaries and demolish conventions, driven as much by a need to prove my worthiness as it was by a pure innovative spirit. Why dismissive critiques, like Hartley's lacerating review, cut so deep is that they tapped into the enduring fear that one day the culinary world would awaken to my limitations and reject me as a charlatan.

Hartley didn't respond with banal platitudes or meaningless reassurances—he just listened to me, holding my raw truths with the same reverence as a chef would his most precious ingredients. He never once took his eyes from mine, and somehow that pale intensity managed to ground rather than discomfit me. In their depths, I saw no judgment or pity, only understanding forged from the smelter of his own life's hardships.

By the end of the evening, I felt as though my body was lighter, as though an invisible burden had slipped from my drooping shoulders—the weight of which I hadn't even been conscious. The two of us had disrobed ourselves of our performer's masks to reveal the authentic human canvases beneath. Not bitter rivals, not even crotchety colleagues—just two remarkably similar souls bent on outpacing the long shadows of our pasts by a simple, indomitable force of will.

As the final tasks were finally done and we were preparing to retreat into the quiet of the night in the city, an unstated truce appeared to have settled between us in the dimmed air of the kitchen. An impasse had broken, a sacred veil lifted to offer a glimpse of the souls that lay beneath the polished personae we had each put on. After tonight, the dynamics would have been changed forever—I could feel the seismic shift carrying within an undercurrent of certainties.

Any judgments or preconceived ideas that might have existed simply disappeared, leaving our essences to become cloaked from one another. The veils of competition, antagonism, and willful nonunderstanding had been pulled away. Only the most uncovered layer of our truths had been revealed recently. For better or for worse, I had the sense that any attempt to re-erect those fallen barriers would be a dispiriting denial. Whatever came afterwards, those ramparts of falsehood were ruins at our feet, the way ahead forever and entirely blocked.

We could not possibly retreat from the very edge of the precipice on which we had been teetering this night. That much was clear beyond any doubt, even if everything else remained incomprehensible.

I had just enough energy to realize that the lonesome kitchen was not my destination, to step into the frail mists of this new world, when fatigue from before came back now with springlike refreshment, as if a serpent had been able to remove its worn skin. The whole world seemed then so disorienting in this new state of being and yet full of possible revelation.

I had no idea where this in-between genesis would ultimately lead Hartley and me, but I dragged the cool, fresh night air into my longing lungs and knew our very coded essences had been permanently refactored by the boundaries we'd traversed together tonight.

It was as though the very tectonic plates undergirding our interactions had been gouged and reforged, leaving us to navigate a startlingly new emotional landscape.

Gone were the staunchly defended boundaries and deeply grooved patterns of behavior that we had each clung to like icy lifelines. Those rigidly demarcated domains of tradition versus avant-garde, discipline versus creative anarchy, no longer easily defined, had faded into a polluted irrelevance. In their place, there bloomed a viridescent frontier of untamed possibilities before us.

I saw this new, very fragile state through the instinctual apprehension of a feral animal peering warily from its protective crouch. Way too many times in the past, any kind of opening for vulnerability or attempt at connectedness was met with a quick rebuttal, punished by Hartley's barbed lashings. Keeping him at arm's length, safely corralled on his narrowly defined side, had been the only way to preserve my own sanity and sense of self-worth.

But now. Something has indefinably changed in the relationship between us. Those territorialities seem almost quaint in retrospect—artifacts of clumsier egos and less fully realized souls. In the stark light of our bare admissions and interwoven truths, such demarcations felt needlessly constrictive. Limiting, even. As if the whole time both of us had been inadvertently hobbling ourselves, our immense creative wellsprings were dammed by the very conceptual embankments meant to contain them.

It was an intoxicating tumult that somehow, with its full visceral experience, was carrying the realization as if it had broken floodgates to let us loose and rush into uncharted waters. Hartley and I began to stray from our predetermined culinary paths; the initially choreographed, so-safe parries and counters transformed into untrammeled collaborative improvisation.

Wild in abandon, we flung painterly streaks of innovation across the blank canvases of our disciplines, once partitioned. And all at once, my innovating flair was bleeding and blending with the traditionalism that exuded from Hartley, each of them two codified rigidities intermingling in some alchemical sympathy. His meticulous Old World techniques anchored my avant-garde gestures, keeping them from fraying into untethered affectation, while my envelope-pushing impulses injected his classics with seething undercurrents of vitality that updated them. The outcome of this creative pollination was of truly transcendental character. Every dish we conspired on took on a lushly tertiary character of its own: part avant-garde mesmerism, part deep-grounded custom, elevated into something miraculously cohered and kaleidoscopic in that Venn space where our talents converged.

We had unlocked multisensory experiences of pure culinary firstness, the likes of which left other cooks and tasters utterly spellbound.

Dishes concocted to blow minds almost as much as they pleased palates: texture tricks; contrapuntal thrusts of contrastive flavors; parfaits of symbolism eddying under the surface, for eyes to really see what lay deep within. Everything that's part of it is calculated to enslave in an almost hypnotic fashion, tugging the diner's attention this way and that, teasing perceptions until they transcend. Hartley and I were rogue culinary deities conspiring in an act of creative magic, drunk on the Promethean high of our collaborative alchemy. We were, in every sense, after that one selfsame unattainable high—the electric transcendence of birthing something vibrantly new, impossibly ambrosial into being from the merger of seemingly incompatible elements. Just like dueling artists, exuberantly riffing off each other's improvisational jazz lines, we egged each other on to ever greater heights of expressiveness and daring.

In the middle of that bacchanal, something akin to time was released from its linear moorings. The world outside our kitchen universe started melting into irrelevance while we channeled whatever divinatory source. Hours blurred imperceptibly; uncounted days bled into one another in the chaotic whirlwinds of inspiration. Where our battling egos once stood so paramount and fortified, time had long rendered them forgotten by this rapturous synergy.

We were not rivals any longer, nor even partners, but rather symbiotic elements of the same creative organism—the cyclone that rips itself asunder in order to glimpse the outer realms of the possible.

We moved in a choreographed unison, as if our molecules knew some deep-down, intrinsic dance that was far too sublime for conscious dictation. Sometimes, I would catch my breath and glimpse our harmonized motions from some out-of-bore movement, mesmerized by the fluidity of it all. Hartley and I were figures sketched, and, dynamic tensions seamlessly gave way to self-same moments of unification. In the dream of our creative ecstasies, I could hardly recall why we were ever adversaries at all. How the need to constantly one-up and discredit each other could once have with such dominance. In this unified congress of artistic moments, the inherent magic of our crafts was made rapturously manifest. Food's power to transcend boundaries, create connections, and shatter limitations self-imposed—it was all laid saliently bare for us as collaborators; the polarities of our worldviews, like long-segregated streams, finally reunited.

It wasn't simply the invention of each new idea that we had dreamt into existence, nor was it that alchemical union of elements working together to change perception; it was a portal to divine possibilities that the very act of culinary achievement may truly become. Boundaries dissolved; territories were entirely forgotten. The last frontier to be charted is that limitless inner realm where creativity and expression hold dominion.

In those transporting moments when the fog of the technical preamble cleared to reveal the absolute primordia of inspiration, I swear I could almost taste the universe's first breath on my tongue. Protogalactic energies billowed through those nascent stars, reborn as flavors too fundamental to be expressed by any terrestrial language or cook's lexicon. Each mouthful is an arcing inversion of the Big Bang—a singularity blooming once more, reforging all of existence from the most modest of culinary components.

Here was art at its most potent and holy—a multi-sensory invocation for remembering our own souls anew: to slough the ill-fitting affectations of civilized selves and taste again, that first inrushing apprehension of Being in its most raw and thunderous glory.

If food is finally the closest thing we have to transcendent sexuality, then Hartley and I were high apostles kneeling in gastronomic congress—making the worldly carnal and un-mating the spirit back into the universal wellsprings from whence it sprang.

And then eventually cool those fevers of revelation, and we'd be left to feel the shudder as we dropped back into the material ledges of our physical vessels. Disoriented seafarers cast from some astral ocean, blinking out the afterburn of the celestial chrysalis in which we'd been wrapped. But in each other's gazes, I swear, was that same unmistakable realization—that whatever regimes we had devotedly served before could never be enough, after tasting the unparalleled majesty of this mutual source. Those valuable symbiotic moments between Hartley and me were too short before this world's gravity re-imposed its dull temporalities on us. But in the reverberations of each creative paroxysm echoing away, I believe a part of that sacred nakedness was seared into our very molecules—all the while reforming us in more subtle, more permanently changed designs that could never be unwoven. If only for those fleeting moments, we had transcended the divides and self-imposed cages keeping our souls quarantined.

In it, the primeval magic of food was made urgently manifest in a way that marked us both as initiates, spelunkers blasted through the veil to glimpse the flashes, pulsing just behind the dull bureaucracy of our waking existences.

We couldn't then forget, ever after, the molten possibilities ever undergirding all of Creation's seeming stasis. Reality itself had become irreversibly more permeable; the demarcations between what was thought to be "possible" and "impossible" were inexorably dissolved.

It was the grand ballroom of a convention center, fairly buzzing with expectancy. The keening hum of voices murmured in excited whispers mixed with the clink of glassware and soft strains of orchestral music. Waiters in crisp black and whites moved easily around the tightly clustered rounds, proffering trays laden with delicate hors d'oeuvres and effervescent aperitifs.

Tonight was the crescendo that our efforts had been building towards with furious intensity for months: the grand opening ceremonies of the Culinary Masters Summit. It is here that the very best and most exacting people in the world will meet up, for the biggest of them all.

It would be a time to see Michelin-starred legends and vaunted critics side by side with the young avant-garde vanguard, as if in one singular celebration of the heights of gastronomic achievement. And Hartley and I were the events' co-hosts, emcees who would quite literally be setting the tone for this illustrious gathering of the culinary elite.

The onus of our role would be hard to overestimate: one misstep, one discordant note, could break the carefully created atmosphere with far-reaching consequences. A single sour reception could tarnish the event's luster and undermine the entire proceeding before it ever began in earnest.

I stood in the wings, looking onto the ballroom floor, and it seemed as if the breath had stayed in my lungs and that my senses were so filled with the smells of the prandial about to unfold. So much had led to this pivotal moment: the grueling creative process, marathon prep sessions, transcendent epiphanies, and soul-baring revelations that had conspired to transmute Hartley and me into—into whatever it was that we had ultimately become to each other. Brothers-in-arms? Intuitive counterweights?

Do we form a set of dyadic catalysts who simply keep pushing each other so as to break through our creative ceilings?

Whatever the exact height, my old enemy was in situ, stoically at my side, his familiar rugged profile silhouetted against the gauzy stage lights. Our previous animosities, once inflamed enough to scorch, now seemed now like echoes of lives long past. In their stead was a bone-deep sensation of haste—somehow, incredibly—fell and landed, caught themselves, on their feet, chests heaving but very much alive.

Equilibrium, the unspoken exhilaration of two daredevils who had fallen off the edge, made it over.

And as the house lights began their slow dimming overture, I glanced at Hartley and felt the seismic mass of that obligation settle in my gut like a lodestone. He just gave me a look out of those pale, implacable eyes that had seemed so chillingly austere in the old days but now simply crinkle at their corners in a way that hints at a wry mirth twinkling behind his inscrutable mask.

"Well, here we go," I muttered softly, for I could now hear the opening strains of the processional music wafting in from the chamber. "All those nights of preparation, all the culinary acrobatics—now it's time to put on one hell of a show."

Hartley gave me one of his patented half-smiles that in some way contained an infinite more degree of warmth than the short expression would be assumed to. Then he just slightly shrugged and clapped me on the shoulder again in a hearty way.

"Not bad for a couple of diametrically opposed culinary zealots who nearly came to fisticuffs on more than one occasion," he said dryly. "If for no other reason, this little partnership ought to lay to rest any lingering doubts we might have harbored about our ability to coexist without turning everything into a scorched battlefield."

I laughed, an unexpected surge of. well, perhaps not fondness, but I dared think of some form of endearment, as the rough notes of self-deprecation echoing through his voice seemed to fill me with. To think that so recently, any word from Hartley's mouth would have been designed purely to raise my hackles. Whereas now, they were nearing comfortable volleys of conversation between friends? Was that what we were? The word seemed unimportant in that catching moment before our entrance onto the international scene.

"Speak for yourself, old man," I chimed in, playfully elbowing him in the ribs, reflexively falling into our newly habituated cadence of teasing repartee. "I had this whole spectacle planned down to the millisecond. It's you who kept dithering over the minute particulars and threatening to throw us hopelessly off schedule."

Hartley chuckled and shook his head resignedly while sticking a hand into one of the pockets of his immaculately tailored tuxedo jacket. He removed it slowly again, his fingers toying with a battered split tin—the same ancient, dented chocolate box that had been my omnipresent companion through our marathon prep sessions. Without thinking, he had flipped back the lid and brought the weathered tin up to his face, inhaling deeply.

Memories came flooding back in a quasi-tactile wave.

Hartley was bent over some sauce, whose reduction had captured his attention in a moment of furrowed contemplation, but his eyes sparkled with a gleam altogether too characteristic of an impish mad genius about to throw the paradigms of reality into a cocked hat once again. The way his hands worked, in perfect movements of each intricate trompe l'oeil plating, made his fingers transport visual illusions, which unveiled hidden depth with each new turn.

An endless parade of samples brought from every highly specialized nook of his extensive culinary arsenal proffered in silence with an unspoken demand for collaborative refinement.

Those scores of moments—once so disorienting and unmooring—had become ritual anchors that helped me map a passage through the seeming chaos. Hartley's strange habits and oddities were no longer irritations or idiosyncrasies to be stamped out, but rather, they had been woven inextricably into my own creative fabric. So much so that I found myself, tin clasped instinctively to my chest, mirroring his savory reverie.

We gazed at each other across that minuscule distance—an entire universe of experiences shared and truths realigned, coursing between us in the suspended breath. Raised one bushy brow in silent question, eyes crinkling fractionally at their corners in a way that relayed everything and yet nothing so very different. It reminded me of our first, tentative reconnection on that long-ago night of marathon prep, how my first resistance had melted inexorably away until we flowed together in near-choreographic synergy, putting on layer after layer of elemental touches and conceptual seasonings, building toward an ever-more-transcendent gestalt synthesis, until finally the very culinary techniques Hartley had so long embodied made some sort of spiritual sense.

CHAPTER 5

Still, the roar of the thunderous ovation was in my ears as I slipped backstage, away from the blinding lights and cacophony of the grand ballroom. My heart was pounding against my ribcage, every single nerve ending—still—buzzingly alive from the sheer adrenaline high. We had managed to pull off the opening ceremonies without a single hitch—Hartley and I—delivering a showstopper that left the culinary elite clamoring for more.

My lungs inhaled deeply, trying to slow down my fast-beating heart as I swept through the dimly lit wings. The high of our achievement washed over me in cresting waves. This was the apex I had always dreamt of: recognition by the most venerated names in the world for my art—indisputable proof that my avant-garde methodologies were warranted, in a place with the sacrosanct traditionalists. A trembling sense of validation, like a tide flowing into my core, threatened to buckle my knees.

I had just begun to make my way into the shadowed recesses when a familiar presence appeared at my side. Hartley. Even in the dim lighting, I could see the sheen of triumphant exhilaration light his craggy features. His slate grey eyes were ablaze, twin stars of barely contained elation boring into me with an intensity that sent a frisson shivering down my spine.

In that suspended moment, everything else seemed to drop away until nothing existed in the world but the crackling energy that was the bridge between our scant space of bodies. Hell, I could swear I almost felt atoms charged and singing in the air, vibrating with the same giddy frequency now thrumming through my veins.

"We did it," Hartley exhaled, his voice a rough scrape of wonder. "I can't believe we actually pulled it off."

The laugh that answered was breathy, giddy, and tinged with disbelief and bone-deep satisfaction—all rolled together in a champagne fizz of happiness. "Was there ever any doubt? We're an unstoppable team, you and I."

Something flickered across Hartley's features then—a shift behind those piercing eyes but totally unreadable. His eyes traveled across my face, mapping every minuscule detail like memorization lines. I was pinned beneath the weight of his scrutiny, breathless and unblinking.

There was another long silence before he spoke again, his voice very low and gravelly. "Stella, I".

Yet whatever it was he intended to say was lost in silence, for our eyes had caught and held, snared in a web of unseen webs. The energy in the room changed in that second, sparking up with a totally new kind of electricity. The air between us was heavy, shimmering with unspoken words and long-repressed desires straining to be let out.

I was drowning in the depths of a stormy gaze, every coherent thought scattering like leaves in a gale. There was a raw, almost feral intensity crackling across his features, a hunger that had nothing to do with food and everything to do with the primal need unfurling in my own belly.

His lips upon mine felt like a dam had just been let loose inside me, with all the longings and desires that had been gnawing at me for months. Heated glances, electric touches, simmering tension between us as we worked side by side in the kitchen—it all coalesced into this one incandescent moment of surrender.

I melted into his embrace, my body molding instinctively to the hard planes of his chest as his strong arms encircled my waist. He devoured me with the same intensity and single-mindedness he poured into his culinary creations, tasting, savoring, and gorging me until I was dizzy and drunk on the exquisite sensations.

My mouth opened to him, and his tongue slid past my lips, dancing with my own in an erotic ballet that left me breathless and aching for more. I tangled my fingers into his hair and tugged him impossibly closer, a needy moan escaping my throat. A low growl is what he replied with, and it ricocheted into my bones, instantly sending a spear of heat to uncurl in my belly.

We stumbled backwards until my spine hit the wall, our bodies never breaking contact. Joseph's hands were everywhere at once, skimming my sides, cupping my breasts, and hitching my thigh over his hip to press his arousal insistently against me. Each touch was an electric spark, fusing my nerve endings into life, making me gasp and writhe wantonly against him.

"Stella," he rasped between open-mouthed kisses at my neck, "I've wanted this. wanted you. for so long. You drive me crazy. your passion, your fire. I can't get enough."

His words were only incendiary, just a repetition of what I had long denied myself. I arched into him, tipping my head back in a wordless invitation. He accepted it, trailing his lips down the column of my throat, teeth grazing my hammering pulse point. Branded by his touch, I felt claimed and possessed, as I'd never been allowed before.

There had been a certain urgency to our coupling—months of foreplay somehow condensed into these stolen moments backstage. Buttons went flying as we tore at each other's clothing, desperate for the slide of skin on skin. Finally, when we came together fully, I cried out from the exquisite sensation of being stretched and filled so completely. He stilled for a heartbeat, foreheads pressed together as we panted harshly, savoring the momentous feeling of our joining.

And then he began to move, and even the ability to form coherent thought had long since flown. There was only the slick glide of bodies, the broken moans and grunts of pleasure, and the rhythmic slap of flesh on flesh echoing obscenely in the charged air. I met him thrust for thrust, nails scoring down his sweat-slicked back as my legs locked around his pistoning hips.

Raw, primal, elemental, a mating unstoppable as the tides. We cleaved to each other in desperation, twin stars collapsing in on themselves in a cosmic explosion. Every nerve in my body was aflame, pleasure building with each pounding drive until it crested over me in a shattering wave. I came with a silent scream, my release triggering Joseph's own as he emptied himself deep inside me with a guttural shout.

We were clung to one another, hearts galloping madly for one another, then slowly falling back from the stratospheric heights with one another. As it was ending, I felt myself shaking under the sheer force of what we had just shared. It was passion such as I have never known; bodies and souls completely enfolded within each other's embrace. I had tasted the forbidden fruit, and now there could be no going back.

The minute hand hung motionless, clamped in the embrace of Joseph's arms, and yet the world seemed to softly return to normal. I understood that everything had irrevocably changed between us. The smoldering embers, so long hidden, had finally been stoked into the roaring inferno that engulfed us, both literally and figuratively.

As the euphoric haze of our passion slowly filtered away, stark reality came crashing over me like a massive wave. I began to inch away from Joseph's embrace; I felt like an icy chill had suddenly struck my skin while his fevered flesh—doubts and insecurities—had begun to creep within the cracks of my afterglow.

What the hell had I done? How could I have let myself get carried away like that, to just give in so completely to the desires I had wrestled with for so long to keep in check? The very same nagging questions that had tormented me for months now arose with vengeance and taunted me with their relentlessness.

Could I really trust Joseph after all this? Our history was a minefield of barbed critiques and bruised pride, a battlefield littered with the shrapnel of our explosive clashes. How could I be sure this wasn't just another fleeting moment of passion, a temporary truce doomed to crumble beneath the weight of our unyielding egos?

I felt the walls I had tried so hard to build around my heart begin to reassert themselves, brick by stubborn brick. Where the vulnerability had been so electric and exhilarating only moments before, now it was like a raw, open wound, a weakness I couldn't afford to let show any further.

Silently, I cursed myself for my folly, for having been lulled by the heat of the moment. I had worked too hard, given too much, and sacrificed too much to have built my reputation and career to throw it all away on a whim. And still, I couldn't shake the memory of how perfectly Joseph's body had melded against mine, the way his touch had sent my soul into an inferno.

I could feel the tug of war within the warring factions of my heart and my mind, and I felt myself retract with every second that passed, the emotional distance between us growing almost exponentially. That had been a defense mechanism—a desperate attempt to shield me from the potential fallout of our reckless actions.

And under the tremendous burden of my insecurities and doubts, I would automatically grab for that old, familiar armor of sarcasm and pretended indifference. It was a well-worn mask, the shield that I donned countless times before the face of emotional uncertainty.

I retreated behind a façade of nonchalance, my lips curling into a practiced smirk as I met Joseph's questioning gaze. The words that spilled from my tongue were sharp and biting, a far cry from the tender confessions we had shared in the heat of passion.

"Well, if that wasn't an unexpected turn of events for the evening, I don't know what is," I tried to put a forced lightness into my voice. "I guess we can chalk that up to the adrenaline rush of doing well at the event."

I could feel the hollowness in my own voice, even as the words left my mouth—the brittle edge that belied the turmoil raging beneath the surface. I was trying really hard to let the way I feel about Joseph sink in, versus the way that we've related for so many years.

How could I truly believe in his sincerity of affection after those many days and nights of tearing each other apart, using words as knives in a never-ending fight for dominance? So many scars from those previous battles were newly formed, the wounds beneath barely healed, covered by the veneer of our newfound connection.

I found it so very hard to understand my emotions of war within me, even after all this time: the undeniable pull of attraction, the simmering heat of desire, and the tenderness that had burst forth in the quiet moments of their collaboration. But, deep down inside, I couldn't shake the fear that this was all just an illusion—a certain kind of illusion that flickers into life through circumstances and would crumble to the ground at the sight of its creator.

The vulnerability that had felt so intoxicating within Joseph's arms was now suddenly looming—a great chasm. A terrifying leap of faith that I wasn't quite sure I was ready to take. This unbearable weight, this burden, would press down on my chest with the mere risk of showing my true self—laying my heart bare, only to have it broken all over again.

And as I wrestled within, trying to hold up a mask of indifference and all the walls, Joseph did not leave my face unattended. He looked like he could see right through to my defenses, his eyes sparkling with comprehension. Somehow, it was disconcerting yet so alluring.

"Stella," he growled, and something about the way he said my name—like a caress, low in his throat—sent shivers down my spine. "I know you're scared. So am I. But what do we have? It's more than just a fleeting moment."

He made a step forward, one hand outstretched to rest on my cheek. I flinched instinctively, my body at war between the desire to lean into his touch and the urge to retreat further into my protective shell. Joseph, however, refused to be deterred.

"I've seen the real you, Stella," he continued, his thumb brushing feather-light circles against my skin. "The passion, the vulnerability, the incredible strength that lies beneath the surface. And I know that our past has been complicated, that we've both made mistakes and hurt each other."

My throat tightened, and I could feel that lump of emotion start to rise unbidden as his words chipped away at my carefully constructed barriers. How could he know, at such a fundamental, intuitive level, the fears that had kept me trapped in this cycle of self-sabotage?

"But I do know that what we found together, what we built, is worth fighting for. I'm not going to let you push me away, Stella. Not now. Not after everything we've been through."

With every word and every gentle caress, I felt my defenses begin to crumble; the walls I had so carefully built began to fall under the warmth of his understanding. He courted me with quiet but steady persistence—a thing that could speak of a deeper commitment, not with grand gestures or dramatic declarations.

"Stella, let me in," Joseph implored, lowering his forehead to rest against mine. "Let me help you face those fears and those insecurities. You don't have to do this alone anymore."

And at that moment, something changed inside of me. The fear that had gripped me so tightly all this while began to dissipate, and in its place, I began to feel a small, gentle spark of hope. In him, a man who truly saw me really saw me, but he decided to stay beside me. A man who would sit out my storms of doubts and fears and peel away my defenses with gentle, unbroken patience.

When I looked into Joseph's eyes, I found a glimpse of my own longing, the desperate desire to connect and be understood. If what was to follow were a journey through uncertainty, even though the ghosts of our tumultuous past still hung over, I knew I could deny the truth that had taken root in my heart no longer.

CHAPTER 6

Standing in the crowded kitchen and overseeing preparations for service, a feeling of creeping dread came over me that settled in the pit of my stomach. We had been negotiating our new place in each other's lives, finding ways to push the taut line that existed between us, both in and out of the kitchen. Nonetheless, in spite of the general irresistible attraction between us, I could not help but get rid of the nagging doubts that now and then lay in the deep recesses of my mind.

That's when I overheard a snippet of conversation between Joseph and one of his long-time chef friends who had stopped by to visit. They were huddled in a corner, their voices low but still audible over the clamor of pots and pans.

"So you and Stella, huh?" The friend said it with a bit of surprise in his voice. "I never thought I'd see the day when Joseph Hartley would settle down with someone, especially not with someone so. different from you."

At the words, my heart clenched, the cold sense of dread seeping like ice into my veins. Different—it was a word that had long haunted me through my culinary career, a never-ceasing reminder that one way or another, I'm, I'm, I would always be an outcast in the world of traditional cuisine.

Joseph's voice was so low that I could've sworn it was just a little bit apprehensive. "Yeah, well, things change, I suppose. You know me, though; I'm always up for a challenge."

A challenge, the words echoed through my mind, resounding against the walls of all my insecurities. A challenge to be faced, a novelty to be tried on before he moved on to the next thrill?

My walls slammed back into place, and the fragile trust we'd been building suddenly became as brittle as spun sugar. How could I have been so foolish, so naive, to believe Joseph could really understand and accept me? We came from different worlds and different philosophies, and no matter how much we tried to bridge that gap, it seemed our differences would always create an insurmountable barrier between us.

So I just watched Joseph say goodbye to his friend and walk back into the kitchen, and it made me want to run, to be anywhere but there, to save myself from the train wreck that was about to occur. I got to work with mechanical efficiency, but to no avail, while a storm of feelings raged beneath the surface.

Joseph got through to me, his hand grazing my arm, and I flinched away instinctively. The hurt that flashed across his face did nothing to help my growing resentment.

"Stella, all good?" he asked, not appearing too happy as his eyebrows knitted together on his face.

I forced a thin smile and made my voice cold with distance. "It's all right, Joseph. We've got much work to be getting on with, so we'll just stick to that, yeah?"

He opened his mouth as though to protest, but I turned away, my attention doggedly fixed on what I had to do. I felt his eyes burning into the back of my neck, but I wouldn't meet his eyes, worried that he would see the cracks in my façade.

Every minute that passed, tension built between us, an almost tangible force that stole the air from the room. Every movement or word was contrived, and every interaction was measured and guarded. I watched the confusion and frustration score into the lines on Joseph's face but could not allow myself to bring out into the open the doubts gnawing at my heart.

It was as the last of the dishes were being cleared away and washed up that it began to feel like the end of the evening; I was exhausted, body and soul. Joseph made another attempt at conversation with me, at bridging the gulf that had somehow come between us, but I half-listened and then weaseled my way out, saying I must go home.

Despair washed through me as I felt the cool night air on my face. Had I just sabotaged the best thing that had ever happened to me, all because of my own insecurities and fears? The thought made my stomach churn, but I buried it, trying to prepare myself for the road of loneliness that surely lay ahead.

Over the next few days, however, I found myself irresistibly pulled back time and again into the deepest recesses of my old patterns of self-protection and emotional isolation. All of my deepest fears and doubts had been triggered by the misunderstanding with Joseph, and I could not shake the conviction that our differences were simply too great to overcome.

I buried myself in my work, working long hours in the kitchen to perfect new recipes and push my culinary boundaries. However, even as I got absorbed in the well-trodden rhythms of chopping, searing, and plating, I couldn't shake off the gnawing emptiness that had taken residence in my heart.

Every time Joseph tried to reach out to me, at some bridge over the growing gap, I pushed him away, the walls between us growing taller and taller with each passing day. I convinced myself that it was all for the best and that I was holding my inevitable heartbreak at bay when he would finally come to understand that I'd never really fit into his world.

So I threw myself back into the apartment, back into the arms of solitude, back into the familiar routines that had always been my sanctuary. Even there, in the quiet stillness of my own space, I couldn't turn off the reruns of all the moments Joseph and I had shared: the laughter and passion, the whispered confessions, and the stolen kisses.

Days were passing by, and I felt myself slowly sinking into a void of numbness and emptiness. I was going through the motions of my life, but things seemed hollow, drained of the spark and joy that had been there before.

My friends and colleagues whispered to each other about the emptiness in my eyes and the razor-sharp edge to my smiles. They tried to reach out to me to give me comfort and support, but I shook them off with the excuse that I was okay, just a little busy with work and concentrating on looking after my well-being.

But okay was nowhere close to the truth. Soon, it became literally cumbersome, as the weight of my fears and doubts seemed to press down each day, suffocating me with a relentless grip. I wanted Joseph back; I wanted him back for being the one who made me feel alive and who understood me, but I could not take that leap of faith toward him.

And so I continued to shove him away, to retreat into the familiar patterns of self-protection and isolation that had always been my armor against the world. I reproached myself, saying it was better to be alone, to shield my heart from possible hurt and brokenness—things one allows when one opens up.

But the truth was, in the quiet times when I'd let myself be really honest, I knew that the only person I was hurting was me. I was closing myself off to the possibility of deep happiness, to a kind of love that could transform my life and make it rich beyond all I could imagine.

I sat in the apartment all alone, staring out at the twinkling city lights like faraway stars, and an emptiness swept over me. I had built a life—a reputation I had worked so hard for—and a professional career I was proud of. But without somebody to share it with, without the warmth, the laughter, and the love I had only just begun to discover with Joseph, it all seemed empty and pointless.

I looked at him from a distance; he had such frustration and hurt clearly written in lines over his face. I had just left him suddenly, leaving work, as he was confused and uncertain about the future that awaited us. I knew my actions were causing him pain, but I seemed unable to break free from the grip of my own fears and doubts.

I watched him throw himself into his work, as sharp and precise as his movements were, yet lacking the spark of passion that had ever drawn me to love him. I wanted to reach out, to bridge this yawning distance between us, but every time I tried, the words stuck in my throat, held back by the walls I had so carefully constructed around my heart.

With each passing day, weeks folding into one another, I could feel our unspoken tensions piling their weight on me, suffocating me with the iron grip that never seemed to let up. I knew I was hurting Joseph. I knew my lack of faith in our love was eating us both up, but it never helped me find the courage to take that leap of faith.

And then one day, something just clicked. I would see Joseph standing there, but there was something about his manner, some new determination in him, as if enveloped in some kind of cape. He would move about with intent, his eyes alight with some fire that had not been there in far too long. It was like I could feel he was up to something, that he was planning some grand gesture to break through my defenses and prove his love, and that he was serious about our relationship.

Part of me was terrified; old fears and doubts were welling in me like a tidal wave, ready to sweep me away. But the other part—that small, stubborn spark of hope—just would not die. It whispered to me and kept reminding me of the deep connection Joseph and I had always shared and of how our love for food and for each other had always been able to transcend our differences.

But as I watched Joseph work, a deep frown of concentration settling on his brow, it came to me that I'd been so caught up in my own fears—in the challenges and obstacles to be fought and overcome, looming ahead—that I had lost sight of the one thing that really mattered: the love we had fought so hard to build; the bond forged in the heat of the kitchen and the depths of our hearts.

I had not been fair to Joseph, since my fears and doubts would rule the relationship, and I just knew it. I had been so scared of being hurt, of being weak, that I had pushed away the one person who had always been there for me, who had believed in me when I had little to no belief in myself.

It then suddenly occurred to me that I just couldn't let my fears hold me back any longer. I had to give a chance to trust in the love that Joseph and I shared, to believe together there was no mountain too high, no river too deep to cross—a future filled with passion, purpose, and endless culinary adventures.

As I watched Joseph at work, his eyes alight with purpose and love, I felt the spark of hope burst into flame within my heart. I did know that the journey ahead would be tough; there would be numerous moments of doubt and ambiguity. I knew our love was worth fighting for, and I knew that the bond we had forged was stronger than any force that tried to tear us apart.

I inhaled, stepping halfway toward Joseph with courage, my heart open; it felt as though I were giving me and my trust to the love that had always been there waiting for me to embrace it. I knew together we could survive anything; our passion for one another and the love of the culinary arts would always light the avenue back home.

The minute I stepped inside the restaurant, my heart sinking from the last two weeks, something very strange started happening to me. It was déjà vu all over again. An empty dining room, the tables laid with crisp white linens and gleaming silverware, just as they had been that night, the first official date with my now ex-husband. Everything was dead quiet, though only the faint strains of music that reached the speakers broke the silence.

Then I saw him. Joseph stood in the middle of the room, his height lit up by the bright candlelight. The sharp suit was hugging his body, his hair done just right, his meeting, and almost drilling into me with such intensity that I had to look away for a moment. In his hand is a single red rose, the petals showing up in bright contrast against the stark white of his shirt.

"Stella," he whispered, barely audible. "I know that lately we've had a tough time with one another, and I know that often I am less than the best at letting you know exactly how I'm feeling. But know that what I feel towards you is real and that I would do anything to prove it."

My heart pounded a little quicker as I took a few more cautious steps forward, my breath catching in my throat. "Joseph, what is all this?" I managed to get out with just a slight quiver in my voice.

He smiled that gentle, soft-curving, half-crooked smile of his, which always made my knees go weak. "This is just my way of showing you how much you mean to me, Stella. Believe me, I am very aware of how much we have varied in different things and how we both have made mistakes. But I am also aware of what we do have, which is worth fighting for: that our love is stronger than anything else that would come between us."

He placed the rose in my hand, the tips of his fingers caressing my skin to the point of making me shiver. "Tonight, I present to you a menu that is dear to my heart, unique to our passions for food, and the individual connection we share. Each plate is a representation of us and our time together, a testimony of love built and the future to come."

Tears pricking in the corners of my eyes and a lump in my throat, I looked up at him. "Joseph, I don't know what to say; this is all so. perfect."

He reached out, cupping my face in his hands, his thumbs gently wiping away the tears that had begun to fall. "Stella, you don't have to say anything. Just allow me to show you how much I love you and how much I believe in us."

With that, he leads me to a small table in the center of the room, pulls out my chair, and helps me to sit. He walks to the kitchen, leaving me completely touched by the feeling of such love and gratefulness for this man who fought so hard to try and bring down my walls to show his commitment to our relationship.

He came back holding a tray full of dishes, one prettier and more decorated than another, and put them before me, beginning to talk softly and somewhat choked about what each meant.

This first dish is a symbol of the start of our journey: the fire, passion, and intense chemistry that, through so much difference and quarreling, brought us to this point. The second dish symbolizes the hurdles we passed, the obstacles in our ways we needed to overcome to be where we are now. And the third dish? The third dish was our future: unlimited, if we are willing to take that leap of faith and believe in our love.

And with every mouthful of food, strong in its flavors and textures, I somehow felt a connection to Joseph; I understood this language of food and how it could relay the sentiments of the heart. And so, with each of us talking, laughing, and crying together, the walls that I had spent so long building began to crumble and fall away like dust in the wind.

It was not in so many physical words, but by the time he held me that close towards the end of the night, whispering words of love and devotion, I knew there was something I had found—something very special, a love never dying but in such a storm coming through even stronger and more beautiful than ever.

I was feeling a wave of emotion wash over me, sitting across from Joseph, the exquisite meal remnants still tingling on my tongue. His grand gesture—so carefully conjured—into meals that seemed to speak words into the tectonic depths of our connection touched me in a manner I hadn't thought possible. My heart swelled with love and gratitude, but tendrils of fear and doubt—the old, familiar ones—crept in, threatening to overshadow the beauty of the moment.

I looked into Joseph's eyes with my own and studied his face, waiting for the smallest indication of doubt or hesitance. "Joseph, I. I don't know what to say. This is just so incredible and perfect. But I can't help wondering: What if it's not enough? What if our differences are just too great to overcome?"

He reached out across the table and took my hand in his. His touch was warm and reassuring.

"Stella, I know you're afraid. I'm afraid, too. But I also know that what we have is worth fighting for and that our love is greater than any obstacle standing in our way."

I could feel the corners of my eyes prick, and my throat got tight with emotion. "But what if I'm not strong enough, Joseph? What if I can't be the person you need me to be, the partner that you deserve?"

His smile was the gentle kind, and it arched his lips in such a way that it skipped my heart a beat. "Stella, you are everything I have needed and more. It is your strength, passion, and determination that I loved—that define who you are."

I inhaled deeply to calm my racing heart. "I know that, Joseph. It's just that I'm so scared that if I let myself get hurt, if I allow myself to be vulnerable, it's going to break me. I've been there before and don't know if I can be there again."

"I know you have been hurt, Stella. I know how you find it hard to lower your guards and let someone into your heart. But please believe me when I say I won't break it again, not on purpose. I will be there, whatever happens." He said it and squeezed my hand, his gaze fixed on mine.

One single tear traced its way down my cheek, my heart filling with love that seemed to consume me. "I want to believe that, Joseph. I want to trust in our love, and in the future we could have together. But I'm so scared of taking that leap of faith, of risking everything on the chance that we might not make it."

He came to my side of the table and knelt by my chair. "Stella, I know it's scary. I know that nothing in life is for sure, and neither are we. But I also know that if we don't take that chance, if we don't open ourselves up to the possibility of love and happiness, then we'll never know what we might be missing out on."

My eyes filled with tears as I looked down at him. "You're right, Joseph. I know you're right. But to let go of those fears, trust that everything will be okay—it's just so hard."

He reached up, cupping my head in his hands, his thumbs softly swiping away my tears. "I know, Stella. I know it's hard, but I'm here for you. Every step of the way. We'll face those fears together, hand in hand. And no matter what, I will love you, and I will always be there for you."

My throat was filled with sobs, and my heart was overflowing with love more than ever before. "I love you too, Joseph. I want to be with you more than anything in the world. I'm just so scared of losing you and losing everything that we have."

He pulled me closer into his arms, holding me tight, his voice low and comforting. "You'll never lose me, Stella. I'm here for you, now and always. And together, we can overcome anything and face any fear or insecurity that might come our way."

So, I held onto him, tears soaking into the fabric of his shirt, deep peace overcoming me as I now knew that the path ahead was not going to be that easy and that moments of wavering and doubt would come. I also knew, however, that with Joseph beside me, I was going to be able to get through and surmount any obstacle that may be in our way.

One last deep breath, a smile that wouldn't hold steady, and I drew back to look him in the eyes. "Okay, Joseph. Let's do this. Let's take this leap of faith. I trust you, and I trust our love. And whatever happens, I know that we'll always have each other."

His smile was laced with wide eyes, sparkling with love and pride. "Of course, Stella. Always. Forever."

CHAPTER 7

I took a sip of my morning coffee and felt it—kind of like a swelling-up of excitement. We had been through so much together, in and out of the kitchen, that it felt like now we were on the edge of something really amazing.

"You want to know what I've been thinking?" I finally spoke out to break the silence that had ensconced both of us in its cozy warmth.

"What if we opened a restaurant together? Someplace where our unique styles and philosophies could be brought together and create something cutting-edge and impossible to forget."

His eyes brightened with a slow smile, and Joseph's lips parted. "I love that idea, Stella. We could take everything we've learned, all the experiences we've had, and pour it into a dining experience that's unlike anything else out there."

I nodded, my thoughts already racing at the possibilities. "Just so. We could put together your traditional techniques with my avant-garde style; create dishes that are familiar yet unexpected at the same time."

He reached across the table and took my hand in his. "And it wouldn't only be about food. We could create an atmosphere that's warm and inviting—a place where people feel like they're part of something special."

A warmth spread through my chest as I smiled. "A place where they feel the love and passion that goes into each and every dish, where they feel the connection between us and the food we make."

Joseph's eyes held mine, intense yet so full of feeling. "Yes, that's what I want, Stella—to do something that would be a reflection of us, of our journey together. A testimony to the power of love and the magic that can happen when two people share a common passion."

My eyes prickled with tears, and my heart swelled with love and thankfulness. There was a pricking of tears in my eyes. "I want that, too, Joseph, more than anything. And I know we can do it together. We can have a restaurant that is not just a place to eat but an experience never to be forgotten."

He raised my hand to his lips and planted a soft kiss on my knuckles. "We'll be able to pour our hearts and souls into every part of it, from the menu to the décor and how service is done. We'll really be able to make a place that defines who we are, more so as chefs than anything else."

I nodded a bit resolutely and with new enthusiasm. "And we do that together, at every step of the way. Whichever challenge comes our way, we meet it face-to-face, together, in love, with a dream in common."

Joseph only smiled at her, his eyes illuminated with pride and adoration. "We do it together, Stella. Always together. And with the blending of our talents and unwavering commitment to one another, I do believe we're going to create something absolutely amazing. A restaurant that will change the culinary paradigm and be a force for good in the lives of all who walk through our doors."

One evening, we sat among swatches and samples on my sofa. Joseph turned to me, clearly in deep thought, and said, "You know, Stella, I've given quite a bit of thought to the future lately, not just the restaurant but our future together."

My heart skipped a beat; a flutter of excitement and nervousness danced in my chest. "Oh, really? What about?"

He took my hand in his, his thumb making gentle circles on my skin. "I know we have been through many things together, and I know that we are still finding things out, but I can't imagine my life without you in it, Stella. I want to spend the rest of my days by your side, building this dream together and experiencing all the joys and challenges that come with it."

I swallowed a hard lump in my throat. "Joseph, are you saying what I think you're saying?"

He smiled, his eyes twinkling with affection and determination. "I'd like to say I'd like to marry you, Stella. I want to be your partner in every single way—to be there for you, love you, and grow old with you. I want to have culinary experiences with you; explore new flavors and new techniques; in short, make memories that will last a lifetime."

My eyes welled with tears, and my love was so deep and true that it nearly made it hard to take a breath. "Oh, Joseph. Yes, yes, a thousand times yes. I want all of that too, more than anything in the world."

He drew me close in his arms and kissed me tenderly and passionately. At length, we both drew back, breathless and giddy, his forehead against mine. "I can't wait to start this new chapter with you, Stella. To plan our wedding, to travel the world together, and to create a life that's rich and fulfilling in every way,

I smiled, and my cheeks were wet from the first joyful tears. "And that we will do, putting all our hearts and souls into this restaurant, putting all our strength into creating something that is a pure reflection of our love and common passion."

"We will be taking inspiration from every place we visit and every culture we explore. We will be back with new ideas and new tastes and incorporate them into the menu in a new and authentic way," he said with eyes full of expectation.

I sighed, leaning into his arms. "And through it all, we'll have each other. No matter what challenge strikes us, no matter how hard it gets, we're always going to be there for each other. Because that is what love is, Joseph. Being there for each other. Always. And forever."

Then he kissed my forehead and whispered with a soft tone, emotion shaking his voice, "That's how I feel, Stella. I promise you, I'll be there to love and support you. Always. You are my everything and my reason to be. And I can't wait to spend the rest of my life showing you just how much you mean to me."

Joseph and I were encapsulated in the creative design of the menu for our new restaurant, right there in the test kitchen. We played around with flavor and technique combinations. Heavy air lay thick with a din of pan sizzles and utensil clatter and the scents of spices and sauces.

At the stove, I'm ladling out a plate of fresh, handmade pasta with a vibrant red sauce. "I wonder how we're going to integrate my love for bold, unconventional flavors with your classic technique," I thought to myself as I sprinkled a handful of fresh herbs over the dish.

Joseph looked up from the cutting board, where he was orchestrating a multi-veggie medley. "I love that, Stella. To take classic dishes and then offer them some new flair—like a deconstructed coq au vin or a sous vide lamb shank with a foam drawing from molecular gastronomy."

That brought the sparkle back into my eyes. "Well, yes, we can play with textures, too, making beautiful dishes that are amazing to the eyes and the palates, like a silky potato purée and a crispy caramelized pork belly."

Joseph nodded and spread a smile across his face. "For instance, we could do summer..." he chuckled to himself, "chilled summer soup made with heirloom tomatoes and just a little smoked paprika."

All of these ideas, half-baked but getting there, somehow came together while we brainstormed and turned into dishes that were the perfectly manifested meeting point between our separate styles and strengths. It was then that my innovative spirit and Joseph's technical precision interwove perfectly to craft a menu that was bold and refined.

"I really do think we have something here," I said, taking in all the various dishes before me. "I mean, a menu that tells a story? It whisks people away on a culinary journey they'll never forget."

Joseph put his arm around my waist and pulled me into his body. "And it's a story we're telling together, Stella. Every dish, every flavor—it's a reflection of us. our partnership—the love and respect we have for one another and our craft.".

I leaned into his embrace, pride swelling through my heart and satisfaction laying gently across the landscape of my soul. "I can't wait to put this out there in the world, Joseph. Show them what we've created together and hopefully inspire them to go out on their own culinary journeys."

Our new restaurant came with great difficulty and struggle. Sometimes, on some days, it did seem like everything went wrong that possibly could. The contractors fell behind time, the equipment got delayed, and hidden expenses started to cast their ugly shadows on the laid-out plans.

I remember very well one very hard day when the pipe broke in the kitchen. After a good two hours of repair work and subsequent successful replacement, the water poured all over the kitchen, and our newly installed household appliances were all in shambles. I felt that I was falling apart, that I should just throw in the towel and give up the dream that was so close but suddenly felt so far away.

And there was Joseph, his constancy an anchor in the insane. He squeezed my hand with an assured look in his steely eyes, as if he were to give me a look full of purpose and love, and he uttered, "We will manage this, Stella." In his voice, he was very calm and reassuring. "Together, we can overcome anything."

And he was right. With every bump along the way and each obstacle, both Joseph and I took it head-on, our common zeal and determination for what we were doing driving us forward. Late nights were spent poring over budgets and timelines, early mornings were spent inspecting construction and deliveries—all this we did together, our bond growing ever stronger with each difficulty we cleared.

There were moments of doubt, frustration, and exhaustion. But then we had each other. One little squeeze of the hand, a whispered word of encouragement, a stolen kiss in the midst of chaos—those are the things that get us through, the little reminders of the love and support that put us on the way to begin with.

Our vision slowly but surely began to take shape. The kitchen was put together, shimmering with evidence of hard work and dedication. The dining room was very warm and inviting, and everything in it was thoughtfully picked out within our shared aesthetic and vision.

We stood there, gazing out at the fruits of our labor, and waves of pride and accomplishment seemed to befall me. We did it. Against all odds, through every single challenge and setback, we brought our dream to life. And we had done it together; the love and partnership were the foundation upon which it was all built.

On the eve of our opening day, Joseph and I sat in the dining room, lit only by the tender light of flames from candles, and realized the warm and intimate atmosphere this created. We had been so absorbed in the whirlwind of preparations—the long list of tasks and details—that we hardly had a moment to catch our breath, let alone to reflect on the journey that had brought us to this point.

It was now, deep in the quiet of the night, with the promise of morning—whether for good or bad—that we finally gave ourselves a moment's peace together. Joseph caught my hand, his fingers laced with mine, and a rush of emotion washed over me.

"Believe it or not, Stella," he leaned in to whisper, his eyes welling with love and pride, "after all we went through—the roller coaster, the highs and lows, the struggles and triumphs—we made it."

I smiled, and my heart swelled with appreciation and love. "It's been quite the ride, eh? From rivals to partners, from enemies to soulmates, go figure."

Joseph laughed gently, his thumb tracing soft circles on the back of my hand. "Of course, I never would have thought so then. But looking back, I realize every step along the way, every twist and turn, brought us to this point. To this beautiful life that we have made together,

I nodded; my eyes were misting with tears. "And it has never been easy. We've had to learn to compromise, to communicate, and to trust in each other and in our love. But most of all, we've let our passion be the driving force. Passion for our craft, for each other, for the life we want to build."

Joseph kissed my hand, then proceeded to lay a kiss on my knuckles. "That's the real recipe for love right there. Passion, compromise, and unwavering commitment to each other. In the kitchen and in life."

I just leaned into him, letting my head rest on his shoulder. "And that's what we've found, Joseph: a love that feeds us, motivates us, and makes us better chefs and people—a love that grows and keeps developing, just like our food."

We sat there in that silent dining room, reminiscing but salient in the promises of what was to come. And then, even before the first light of dawn had pierced the window in a dance heralding the arrival of a new chapter, I was sure that whatever came next, whatever lay in our future to challenge us, we would meet it. With the unshakeable passion with which love had brought us to this very moment.

The night of our grand opening in the restaurant is something that I will never forget. It was filled with the sound of clinking glasses and the murmur of voices in the dining room, while the kitchen exuded a delightful smell.

Joseph and I walked the room, hosting the guests and then telling stories, heart-to-heart, full of pride and excitement. Months of work, late nights, early mornings, blood, sweat, and tears—it had all added up to this. And looking all around at the smiles and plates filled with beautifully crafted food, I knew it had all been worth it.

And then the reviews started to trickle in, one better than the next. Comments on the innovative menu and the seamless blend of classic techniques with modern flavors. Noted was the chemistry between Joseph and me that was present in each dish, as if each dish was prepared with the love and passion he and I obviously shared.

Diners raved about how the food swept them away to another place and how the setting and the service made them feel like they were part of something truly special. They just went on and on about the magic that happens when two very gifted chefs get together, when strengths and perspectives from each blend to create something truly special.

The night had gone on, the last stragglers had left, and it was just Joseph and me in the kitchen, our bodies still pumping with the adrenaline of the evening. We were staring at each other as the realization of what we'd done started to settle in.

"We did it," I breathed, my voice thick with emotion. "We actually did it."

Joseph had pulled me to him, and our laughter mingled together. "We did it together, Stella. Just like we always said we would."

And here we were amidst all those tools of our trade, evidence of our shared passion and dedication, and I felt something close to pure, unadulterated joy wash over me. What we worked so hard on, putting our hearts and souls into. And this is just the beginning.

Everything was possible with Joseph by my side. We found the recipe for success, both in the kitchen and in life. It struck a perfect balance between passion and partnership, innovation and tradition, and love and commitment.

We walked out into the night, two in hand, my mind on fire with anticipation for the future—the culinary adventures we'd undertake, the new flavors and techniques we would discover, the mark we would leave upon the industry that we both loved so much.

More than anything, I was filled with a huge sense of gratitude for the journey that brought us to this moment, the challenges we had to go through, the lessons we had to learn, and the love that we found in each other—it brought us here to this beautiful life we have made together.

Walking back home with the city lights all twirling around me, I knew that this was just the first step towards a lifetime of culinary triumphs and personal joys, of passion, of love, and of the endless possibilities that lay ahead. Together, Joseph and I redefined the culinary scene, pushed all boundaries, and created a legacy that has outlived us.

But for the time being, we would bask in this moment—this remarkable achievement that told the story of our love and our shared vision. We would carry on the glory of success and tarry for all the beautiful moments just ahead. Together, in the kitchen and in life.

About the Author

Lila Vex is an emerging talent in the world of romance literature, captivating readers with her tales of love and adventure. With her skillful storytelling and vibrant characters, she transports readers to enchanting worlds where love conquers all.

When she's not immersed in writing her next romance novel, Lila enjoys exploring the great outdoors and indulging in her love for travel.

Stay updated on Lila Vex's latest releases and projects by visiting her website.

Read more at https://www.lilavex.com/.